The Call of the Wild

Retold by
Stewart Ross

Illustrated by
Vince Reid

ARCTURUS

For Zac Ross, with love—SR.

For Bob, my Dad—VR.

ARCTURUS

This edition published in 2018 by Arcturus Publishing Limited
26/27 Bickels Yard, 151–153 Bermondsey Street,
London SE1 3HA

Writer: Stewart Ross
Illustrator: Vince Reid
Designer: Jeni Child
Editor: Sebastian Rydberg
Art Director: Jessica Crass

ISBN: 978-1-78828-690-9
CH006284NT
Supplier 24, Date 0318, Print run 6734

Printed in Malaysia

Contents

CHAPTER 1

Kidnapped!

Buck was like no other dog. His huge size came from his father, a St. Bernard. His mother, a clever sheepdog, had given him his brains. His many adventures began with the men who owned him. But in the end, Buck ran wild and free.

Our story opens in the warm and sunny state of California. Buck was born there

into the wealthy household of Judge Miller. His early days were comfortable and easy.

The judge's large house was approached through wide gates down broad drives. His lawns were neat, his gardens tidy, and his fields rich. All this, Buck enjoyed.

He played on the grass and went hunting with the judge's sons. In the evenings, he lay before a roaring fire and dreamed.

The judge's other dogs respected Buck. As well as being bigger and stronger than them, he was also more intelligent. He was their lord, the king of the judge's estate. He understood things, almost like a human.

Almost—but not exactly. He could not, for example, read the newspapers. Had he done so, he would have known trouble was brewing. In the far north, in the land of ice and snow, men had discovered gold.

The only way to travel over the snow of the distant gold fields was by sled. There were no trucks or tractors, and horses could not survive in the cold. Only teams of dogs could manage the heavy loads.

But tie a terrier or a poodle to a sled, and nothing happens. They are too small and weak; besides, they cannot stand freezing temperatures. Sled drivers need heavy dogs with strong muscles and thick, furry coats that keep out the cold.

Buck was one of these dogs. Manuel, one of the judge's gardeners, realized this, and a wicked thought entered his head.

Manuel had a large family and earned just about enough to feed them all. But he needed more. He was a gambler, and every time he played cards, he lost money.

He grew desperate. "Come on, Buck," he called one evening, when no one was around. "We're going for a walk."

Buck trusted Manuel and set off at his side through the orchard. At a small train station, they met another man who paid Manuel money.

Only now, when a rope was slipped around his neck, did Buck sense that something was wrong.

He bared his teeth and growled.

Buck had always trusted humans. But when Manuel handed the rope to the other man, Buck rebelled. Deep inside him, a voice whispered, *This is not right! Danger!*

He leaped up at the stranger, aiming to grasp him by the throat. The man was waiting for him. In the air, the rope tightened around Buck's neck as the man spun him around. He smashed Buck to the ground.

Half choked, Buck was lifted into a train wagon. He was furious! Never in all his life had he been treated so badly. When one of the

men guarding him came close, his anger exploded.

With a furious snarl, he sank his teeth into the man's hand. The fellow yelled with pain, but Buck let go only when the rope around his neck was so tight, he couldn't breathe.

To stop him from attacking again, the guards locked him in a wooden cage. In vain, he snapped and charged at the bars. For two days, as the train rattled north, he had neither food nor water.

Buck's eyes grew as red as the anger within him. Gone was the house dog. In his place stood a savage beast that even the judge would not have recognized.

When the train stopped, the wagon door opened, and four men climbed in.

"That's some dog," said one of them when he saw Buck.

"Sure is," said another. Buck, crimson-eyed and full of wrath, snarled. "And looks pretty dangerous, too," added the man.

They lifted Buck's cage and carried it to a small yard. High walls surrounded it on all sides—there was no way out. The men placed the crate on the ground and sat on the top of the wall to see what would happen.

A large man in a sloppy red sweater came in and shut the gate behind him. In one hand, he held a hatchet, in the other a stout wooden club. He smiled and walked over to the cage.

Buck threw himself against the bars. *Another cruel man come to mock me,* he thought. *I'll show him!*

The man in the sloppy sweater chopped open the cage with his hatchet. "Right, you red-eyed devil," he muttered, "come on out!" As he spoke, he dropped his hatchet and took the club in his right hand.

Buck stepped out of the broken cage and sprang. All one hundred and forty pounds of him flew straight toward the man's neck.

Crash! When Buck's jaws were inches from the throat of the man in the red sweater, something cracked into his head. It was the club.

Buck landed heavily on his side. No one had ever hit him like that before, and he didn't know what was happening. He rose and launched himself at the man a second time.

Crash! Once more, the club smashed into Buck's head. He fell to the ground, rose, and attacked again. And again. Each time, he was hammered down, until finally, he passed out.

He was beaten, and he accepted it. He was not broken, but he was too intelligent to attack when he knew he couldn't win. Later, he saw a dog who didn't understand this. The dog was brave but foolish—and he was killed.

Buck had learned his first lesson in a world where only power mattered: A man with a club would always be his master.

Now that the man in the red sweater had shown who was boss, he patted Buck's head and gave him water and meat.

"You've learned your place, Buck," he said in a friendly voice. "So, be a good boy, and everything will be all right."

CHAPTER 2

The Law of Club and Fang

Now that he had learned the law of the club, Buck was ready for work. He was bought by two tough Canadians, Perrault and François. Their job was delivering letters to the gold fields.

Buck hadn't met men like them before. They were as hard as the ice over which they journeyed, but they were fair. If the dogs behaved and worked hard, they were fed and looked after. But woe betide the weak or lazy ones!

Perrault and François carried the letters hundreds of miles by sled. They'd come south to Seattle to buy new dogs for their team. As well as Buck, they bought a gentle Newfoundland dog named Curly.

They trekked back to Alaska by sea. On the boat, Buck met two huskies of the sled team: Spitz, the leader, and the miserable Dave. Buck quickly learned to ignore Dave— and to watch out for the leader. Spitz was clever, crafty, and merciless.

Buck learned something else. The moment his feet touched the ground in Alaska, he leaped into the air. What was this strange, cold white stuff on the ground? It was his first snow.

Life in Alaska was merciless. Among dogs, the law of the fang said only the tough survived, and Buck grasped it immediately. Gentle Curly did not.

They were camped near a store when Curly approached a husky to say hello. The savage beast turned in a flash and struck with its fangs. Curly's face was torn open from eye to jaw.

Immediately, thirty or forty other huskies gathered. They formed a silent circle around the two fighting dogs, waiting for one to fall. Wounded and angry, Curly attacked. The husky dodged aside and slashed at her again.

Curly charged a third time. The husky, an experienced fighter, was waiting. As

Curly reached him, he batted against her with his chest, knocking her to the ground.

This was what the pack had been waiting for, and they leaped upon Curly before she could get back her feet. She screamed for help, but none came. Buck watched—and remembered.

He had seen the law of the fang in action: A dog that went down in a fight was finished. Buck also remembered something else. Spitz had watched the scene with a smile on his face. From that moment, Buck despised him.

Perrault and Francois got going at once. They tied their nine dogs into a harness, or "traces." These were fixed to a line attached to the sled. Spitz, the lead dog, was at the front.

Buck hated the idea of traces. How could a king be forced to work like a horse? But he remembered the man in the red sweater and kept quiet.

He learned fast. The command "mush"

meant go, and "ho" meant stop. If he made a mistake, he felt Perrault's whip. And dogs who did not pull their weight felt Spitz's teeth.

They rose at dawn and ran all day. Up mountain passes and over frozen lakes they went, on and on. On good days, they covered forty, fifty, even sixty miles.

On his first night, Buck wandered about looking for somewhere to sleep. The other dogs were in snug burrows that they had dug under the snow. When Buck learned their trick, he curled up and slept like a puppy.

His muscles became iron hard. His mind hardened, too. He forgot the ways of the soft south. Slowly, he was returning to the wild ways of dogs long ago, before humans had tamed them.

At the end of the day, Perrault and François fed the dogs before themselves. This was the custom of the men of the north. Without their dogs, they would die.

But a dog was useful only if it worked. Buck was shown this when Dolly, one of the quieter dogs, went mad. She ran about wildly, refusing to do what the men or Spitz ordered. One blow from Perrault's hatchet ended her life.

Once again, Buck watched and learned. He now knew how to bite ice from between his toes and how to break the ice on a lake to get a drink. He ate anything and everything.

His senses sharpened. At night, he woke at the slightest sound —was that falling snow or a prowling enemy? Whatever happened, he would survive.

Back in the south, Buck had been a chief. All the judge's other animals had recognized that Buck was born to lead.

But now, in the dog team, someone else was leader. Whatever his feelings, Buck had to follow Spitz. Yet, Buck knew—as did Perrault, François, and all the other dogs—that there could not be two leaders in the same team.

One of them had to go.

When Buck and Spitz first fought, Perrault and François forced them apart with clubs. The next time they fought, there were neither men nor clubs. It was a fight to the death.

After supper one evening, a rabbit darted in front of the team. Off they went in pursuit. A pack of huskies joined in, fifty dogs after one small rabbit.

Buck took the lead. To begin with, Spitz followed him. Then, guessing where the

rabbit was headed, he moved to ambush it.

Spitz waited, his fangs gleaming ivory white in the moonlight. When Buck and the rabbit appeared, Spitz caught the rabbit and killed it.

Buck did not stop. Into Spitz he crashed, sending both dogs rolling in the snow. They sprang to their feet, and the fight began. In silence, the pack formed a circle around them and watched.

Spitz had experience, but Buck had imagination. After Spitz had withstood his straightforward attacks, he changed tactics. Darting in upright, he dived down at the last moment and bit deep into Spitz's leg.

Crack! The bone snapped. Limping, Spitz fought on. But his time had come. Buck knocked him down, and the pack closed in. Buck was a king once more.

CHAPTER 3

The New Leader

"What did I tell you?" said François the next morning when he saw that Spitz was missing. "That Buck is a devil."

Perrault looked at Buck's many wounds and observed, "But that Spitz sure gave him a fight. Anyway, we now need a new leader."

To Perrault, the obvious choice was the oldest dog. This was the fierce, one-eyed Sol-leks. But when he moved Sol-leks to the front, the dog did not want to go. It was soon clear why: Buck sprang at him and drove him back.

Perrault pulled Buck to one side and tried again. The same thing happened. "Right, Buck," growled Perrault, "I'll teach you a lesson!" He picked up his club.

Buck remembered the man in the red sweater and backed away. When Perrault advanced, Buck retreated, snarling. But once the man's back was turned, Buck moved up again, growling at Sol-leks.

François came to help. It made no difference. Sol-leks would not go into the traces of the lead dog, and Buck would not come near a man with a club. After an hour, the men gave up, threw down their clubs, and gave the position of lead dog to Buck.

Perrault and François knew Buck was intelligent, and they knew he was powerful. But he was young and had not been in the north for long. Moreover, he was not a husky, the usual sled dog.

Nevertheless, what he did was amazing.

In next to no time, he had the whole team obeying him. Even Joe, the fiercest of them, cowed down when Buck snapped at him. They understood that their new leader was a very special dog.

Life became easier for Perrault and François. The team got into their traces without fuss and pulled harder than ever. In the evenings, when the day's work was done, they behaved.

Buck was proud of his dogs. More than that, he felt at home in the frozen wastes. It was as if he had known the snowy

mountains and dark pine forests all his life. They seemed to call to him—the call of the wild.

He had a strange dream, too … *He is in a cave. Beside him, a primitive man squats beside a fire. The man and he are friends. Outside, beyond the mouth of the cave, the eyes of dangerous creatures glint in the firelight.*

The team grew better and better. When two new huskies were added, Buck brought them under control at once. On they sped.

"There's never been a dog like that Buck," cried François. "He must be worth one thousand dollars!"

They finished the trip in record time, at an average of forty miles a day. In the bars of the town, Perrault and François stuck out their chests and boasted. "We are the best!" they crowed.

The journey had left the dogs exhausted. When Perrault and François received orders to make another trip at once, they were heartbroken. Buck and his team were in no state to go on, and they had to be sold. When François said goodbye to Buck, he threw his arms around the great dog's neck and cried.

Two Scottish men bought the team.
Not long afterward, they set off along the
mountain trail that the dogs had just come
down. The load was heavy, and the way was
rough. There were no records this time.

Snow fell every day, making the sled
hard to pull. The drivers grumbled, and
the weakened dogs whined in their sleep.
Joe and Sol-leks were grumpier than ever.
The future looked grim.

Dave was now very sick. The men examined him but could find nothing. Something was wrong inside, they said.

He had no energy and cried out in pain when the sled suddenly stopped or started. After a week, he was falling over while they ran.

The driver couldn't let the other dogs drag Dave with them. He cut him out of the traces and moved Sol-leks into

his place. Dave's pride was badly hurt. He felt he had failed, and whimpered and growled with shame.

When the sled started, he tried to run beside Sol-leks and nip his heels. He moaned in agony at the effort. When his strength ran out, he lay in the snow and howled.

Somehow, he made it to the next camp. The following morning, out of pity, the driver put him back in his old traces. It was hopeless. He fell and the heavy sled ran over his leg.

The next day was Dave's last. When he was too weak to move, the sled left without him. After going a little way, the driver stopped, and his companion went back to the camp. A shot rang out. All the dogs knew what had happened.

When they reached their destination, the team could hardly stand. Their feet hurt dreadfully. Buck's weight had fallen drastically. The other dogs were almost skeletons.

For months, they had toiled in the traces. Day after day, they had risen at dawn, heaved a heavy sled all day, and gone to sleep in the snow. They needed good food and a month's rest.

The drivers were exhausted, too. They expected a long break in which to relax and get their strength back. It was not to be.

New orders said a pile of fresh letters had arrived, which had to be delivered immediately. *And if your dogs are too tired, sell them and buy new ones. Delivering letters is more important than dogs.*

The Scotsmen had no choice. Buck

and his team, thin and worn out, were sold for next to nothing. Those who knew the business said it was a scandal.

Buck inspected his new owners carefully. They were Americans from the south, not used to the ways of the icy north. Their clothes were smart, their hands soft, and their eyes watery. Buck did not like the look of them at all.

CHAPTER 4

Rescue

Now began the very worst period of Buck's life. His new owners, the middle-aged Charles and the nineteen-year-old Hal, were hopeless. They knew nothing about sled travel and nothing about dogs.

To make matters worse, Charles and Hal thought they knew about everything. They used the words "mush" and "ho," but they had no idea about feeding the team properly. Hal, the driver, decided all problems could be solved with his whip.

Charles had his wife, Mercedes, with him. She was an empty-headed, vain young woman. She understood the ways of the north even less than the men.

Things went badly from the very start.

The three explorers piled a mountain of luggage high on the sled. Most of it was Mercedes's clothes. "That load's too heavy," one onlooker pointed out.

Hal ignored him. "Come on—mush!"

Buck and his team heaved, but the sled wouldn't move. Hal slashed them with his whip. "I said *mush*!" he yelled.

The dogs tried again, and slowly, the heavy sled started to slide forward.

An old-timer muttered, "Those fools sure won't get far. You watch."

The old-timer was right. The sled moved slowly along the trail until it came to a bend. Here, the track was higher on one side. The sled leaned, wobbled, and crashed right over into the snow.

When they finally got the sled and luggage back to base, Mercedes burst into tears. She couldn't take all those clothes—there was room for only one or two items.

The sled was loaded up once more, but it wasn't much lighter. The reason was Mercedes. Instead of walking beside the sled, like other companions, she demanded to ride on it with the bags.

The exhausted dogs made slow progress. Hal's whipping and swearing didn't help—nor did his feeding.

Experienced drivers knew how long their journey would take. They packed the right amount of food, so the dogs had the correct rations and wouldn't go hungry.

Hal took enough frozen fish for his dogs to have a good meal every day. However, hoping to make them go faster, he increased their daily ration. The idea was a failure. By the halfway point of their journey, all the dog food had gone.

Starved and hardly able to walk, the dogs struggled on. Meeting a stranger, Hal swapped his revolver for dried horse hide and fed it to the team. It was tough and contained very little goodness, but the dogs ate it all the same.

There were now only five of them left. When he had his revolver, Hal had shot those too sick or too tired to work. After the gun was gone, he killed them with his hatchet. Those that remained, he whipped and clubbed.

In this state, more dead than alive, the team stumbled into the camp of John Thornton. John had lived in the wilds for years, and he knew its ways as well as anyone. When he saw the miserable train of dogs collapse before him, he breathed deep and frowned.

"So, where are you folks headed?" he asked.

"Down there," replied Hal, pointing to a frozen lake below them.

John Thornton frowned again. "I wouldn't do that," he advised. "The ice is paper-thin right now. It won't hold your weight."

Hal laughed. "Nonsense! We haven't come all this way to listen to some scare story." He turned to the dogs. "Mush!"

Buck did not move.

The whip flashed out. Thornton pressed his lips together but said nothing. Sol-leks crawled to his feet, followed by Jo and two others. But Buck just lay there.

The whip cut into him. Thornton stood and walked up and down anxiously. Buck neither whined nor moved.

Hal seized his club and rained heavier blows upon Buck's wasted body. He could have risen like the others, but he had decided not to. He had made up his mind—enough was enough.

Perhaps there was something else, too? As the team had crossed a frozen lake earlier in the day, Buck

had felt the thin ice cracking. Maybe he
understood the peril of going on? As the
blows fell, he felt strangely numb.

Suddenly, John
Thornton yelled,
sprang forward, and
knocked Hal over.
"If you hit that dog
again, I'll kill you,"
he gasped. Mercedes
screamed. Charles did nothing.

"He's my dog," snarled Hal, drawing
his knife. "I'll do what I want with him."

Thornton knocked the knife from
Hal's hand. Stooping, he picked it up
and cut Buck free from the traces.
Hal shrugged. Minutes later, the three
humans and their pitiful team headed
down the trail toward the frozen lake.

Buck and Thornton watched the sled make its way slowly down the slope. The man sighed and shook his head. With his eyes still on the doomed explorers, he began to run his hands over Buck's body.

The poor creature was in a terrible state. Thornton's fingers, rough but skilled, found almost no flesh on the skeleton. There were terrible, swollen bruises and cuts from the whip, but happily, no bones appeared to have been broken.

By the time Thornton had finished his examination, the sled was at the edge of the lake. Man and dog knew what was sure to happen. The team advanced gingerly across the thin ice, then abruptly stopped.

The back end of the sled dipped down, lifting the dogs. Mercedes's scream carried through the clear spring air like a whistle. Charles turned and tried to run back.

It was too late. A whole plate of ice gave way with a crack that echoed off the mountainsides. The men, the woman, the dogs, and the sled disappeared into a wide, dark hole. Nothing rose to the surface.

Thornton and Buck looked at each other. "You poor devil," John said.

Buck licked his hand.

CHAPTER 5

John Thornton

That spring, as the days grew longer and warmer, Thornton nursed Buck back to health. In return, Buck loved the man who had saved his life and liked nothing better than to lie by the fire, hour after hour, watching Thornton's face.

They shared little habits. The man held Buck's head between his hands, rocked him back and forth, and called him special names. Buck took Thornton's hand between his teeth and held it there, tight. It was his way of saying, *I love you, Master.*

Skeet, Thornton's
little Irish setter,
helped Buck's

recovery. Every morning after breakfast,
she licked his wounds. It was like a cat
licking a kitten.

Thornton had a third dog, half
bloodhound, half deerhound. Though
huge, he never turned angry with Buck. All
three animals were Thornton's children,
and his love spread through them all.

When he had recovered, Buck had a
chance to show his master how much he
cared for him. They were in a bar when
a rough bully punched Thornton. With a
mighty roar, Buck was on him, grabbing
him by the throat. He was pulled off before
he killed the man, but he was now famous
throughout all the gold-mining country.

That fall, Buck came to Thornton's rescue in quite another way.

Thornton and his partners, Pete and Hans, were taking their boat down a fast-flowing river. Thornton was on board, drifting with the current. Hans, who was on the bank, steadied the boat with a rope.

The line jerked suddenly. The boat lurched and threw Thornton into the water. The current, stronger than any man, carried him swiftly downstream in the direction of deadly rapids.

Buck immediately leaped in and swam to his master. When he felt Thornton seize his tail, he headed back toward the bank. But the current was too strong for him. Grabbing hold of a rock, Thornton ordered him back to the shore.

Thornton was safe for the moment,

but his strength was failing fast. As Buck
reached the bank, Hans tied a rope
around him and sent him back into the
swirling waters. Bravely though he swam,
he could not reach his master.

Hans pulled him back and tried again.
Battered by rocks and half-drowned, Buck
made it to Thornton's side. The man fixed
his arms around Bucks's neck, and Hans
heaved. More dead than alive, Thornton
and Buck finally reached the bank.

Thornton was mighty proud of Buck. One day in a saloon, he met Matthewson, a man with a big mouth and loads of gold.

"My dog," he boasted, "can start a frozen sled of seven hundred pounds in weight and pull it for one hundred yards."

"Bah!" exclaimed Thornton. "My Buck can do that with a thousand pounds."

"Never!" sneered Matthewson.

"What d'you bet?" retorted Thornton.

Matthewson produced a bag of gold worth a thousand dollars. Thornton did not have that kind of money, but he was too proud to back down.

The sled was loaded with a thousand pounds and the course measured. Buck, sensing the excitement, took his place.

"If you love me, Buck ..." whispered Thornton in his ear. Buck understood.

"Gee!" cried Thornton. Buck heaved the sledge to the right.

On the command "Haw!" it went left and was free of the ice.

"Now, mush!" shouted Thornton.

Inch by inch, the sled moved forward. Soon, it was running smoothly. When it reached the hundred-yard mark, the crowd went wild. No one had ever seen anything like it. Thornton embraced his beloved Buck and cried with pride and joy.

The story of Buck and the thousand-pound sled spread far and wide. Thornton was offered huge amounts for his remarkable dog. But Buck wasn't for sale.

Thornton used the money he made from the bet to pay off his debts. He was now free to explore. With his companions, Hans and Pete, he set off into the empty land of lakes and mountains in the east.

Here, it was said, lay a great mine full of purest gold. No one knew exactly where the mine was—*in the east* was all Thornton had heard. But he was determined to find it.

What a time it was for Buck! There was no speeding along frozen trails. Instead, they went where their fancy took them, on and on, through lonely passes and beside still lakes. They hunted for food and camped wherever they wanted.

Once, they found a trail and followed it through the woods. All of a sudden, it stopped. It had come from nowhere and gone nowhere.

Another time, they came across a log cabin. Inside were rotten blankets and an ancient, rusty gun. There no other signs of life. Human beings had not been there for over a hundred years.

For months they journeyed. Summer turned to fall, fall froze to winter, winter melted into spring. Eventually, in a broad valley, they found the gold they were seeking.

It gleamed like butter in the sunshine. The men toiled day after day collecting it into sacks. They had never worked so hard in all their lives.

There was little for Buck to do, though he felt he was back where he belonged. This land, the primitive land of forest and fang, was his land.

At night, he dreamed of himself and the wild man in the cave. By day, he felt a strange call growing within him. *Come away*, it said. *Return to the wild.*

Buck obeyed the call. He went off on his own, loping through woods and beside clear streams that ran down long, empty valleys. And one day, in this wilderness, he met a wolf.

They did not fight. Instead, after a while, they became friends, and the wolf asked Buck to follow him. They ran together for miles until Buck felt another call: his love for John Thornton.

He stopped and turned back. When the wolf saw this, he sat down, raised his head to the stars, and howled.

CHAPTER 6
Return to the Wild

The man in the red sweater had taught Buck the law of the club. Spitz had taught him the law of the fang. After that, he was no longer a pet.

However, Buck loved John Thornton and would have died for him. But not for anyone else. He allowed Thornton's friends to pat his head, but he did not enjoy it.

He was a killer. He had killed Spitz and other dogs because he had had no choice. It was the primitive law: In the wild, it was kill or be killed.

And Buck killed often now. The men had no need to feed him, for he hunted his own food. Rabbits, birds, fish—with stealth and strength, he caught and killed them.

Once, to test his hunting skills, he brought down a giant moose. The beast was many times bigger and stronger than him. One kick of its hooves would have slain him. Each of the fourteen spikes on its antlers was like a spear.

Buck knew this and kept his distance. For four days, he hunted the great beast until it fell to its knees exhausted. Then, Buck went in for the kill.

For a day and a night, feasting and sleeping, Buck stayed beside the body of the moose he had killed. He then set out for home and John Thornton. At first, the journey was easy. But as he got nearer the camp, he sensed something was wrong.

There was a message in the air. The birds spoke of it, the squirrels chattered about it. Finally, three miles from the camp, Buck picked up the scent. Someone else had been this way.

From the valley came the sound of strange singing. Thornton and his men did not sing like that. Buck crept closer.

He passed the bodies of dogs killed by arrows. The singing grew louder until he came to the edge of the clearing where Thornton's cabin stood. It was a wreck.

Nearby, Yeehat warriors were dancing and singing. This was their land. Their families had lived here for thousands of years. Men like John Thornton had no right to be there, and they had been killed. It was the law of the wild.

For the last time in his life, Buck didn't stop to think. Fury seized him. He uttered a terrifying growl and charged upon the Yeehats.

Later, the Yeehats said the Evil Spirit had attacked them. That was how they remembered Buck. To them, he was not a wolf or a dog. He was a roaring, raging monster.

He sprang at the Yeehat chief and tore out his throat. Without a pause, he killed a second man, then a third. Warrior after warrior fell before his terrible fangs.

Packed together, the Yeehats panicked. Buck moved so fast that they could not shoot at him. When they tried, their arrows hit their own men. Those who were left alive fled into the forest.

When tired of chasing them, Buck returned to the camp. He found the bodies of Hans, Pete, and the dogs, but there was no sign of John Thornton.

Buck followed his master's scent to the edge of a pool. The water was dark, cloudy, and deep. In there, Buck knew, lay the body of the man he loved.

Buck sniffed the dead Yeehats. He was proud to have killed the noblest prey of all. From this time forward, men would not frighten him.

Now that Thornton was gone, men would not own him, either. At nightfall, he retired to the edge of the forest.

Buck had left the world of men, but the animal world had yet to accept him.

He stopped in the middle of a clearing and waited. Silently and stealthily, the wolf pack came out of the darkness.

For a moment, the creatures hung back. Facing them, Buck stood huge and magnificent in the moonlight. One of the pack leaders attacked first, leaping straight at Buck. The wolf's neck was broken before he reached the ground.

Three other wolves came forward. All were soon in retreat, blood streaming from deep slashes. Next, with a snarl, the whole pack launched itself at Buck.

He was too intelligent for them and too quick. Left and right, he snapped and clawed. To give himself height, he rose above them on his hind legs. When they threatened to get behind him, he retreated into a corner.

He was now protected on three sides.
There, he stood and held off the wolves
for half an hour. In the end, they backed
away. Buck had won.

Cautiously, an old, lean wolf came
forward. Buck recognized him as the
wild brother he had met in the forest.
The two animals whined softly at each
other as their noses touched.

Buck was now accepted by the pack. When the old wolf sat and howled at the moon, the others did the same. So did Buck. And when the leaders ran off into the forest, Buck ran with them.

He had answered the call of the wild.

How long Buck ran at the head of the pack, we will never know. But it was long enough for a legend to be born. Yeehats and hunters speak of a huge Ghost Wolf, bigger than anything ever seen before. It steals from their camps and kills their dogs.

There are stories, too, of hunters who never return. Their bodies are found in the forest. All around are the footprints of an enormous wolf.

Men stay away from the valley where the Yeehats had met with the Evil Spirit.

But one animal still ventures there. Every summer, when the days are long and warm, he returns alone to that empty place.

He stands for a while, thinking. Then, he sits and howls a single, long, mournful howl. It is Buck's farewell to the man he loved, the man he will never forget.